Who Wants a DRAGON?

For Gabriel the Bold!
With love from your dad

For Molly the Menace!
With love from your fairy godmother, Lindsey

ORCHARD BOOKS
96 Leonard Street, London EC2A 4XD
Orchard Books Australia
32/45-51 Huntley Street, Alexandria, NSW 2015
First published in Great Britain in 2004
First paperback publication in 2005
ISBN 1 84362 493 1 (hardback)
ISBN 1 84362 494 X (paperback)
Text © James Mayhew 2004
Illustrations © Lindsey Gardiner 2004
The rights of James Mayhew to be identified as the author and
Lindsey Gardiner to be identified as the illustrator of this work have been asserted by them
in accordance with the Copyright, Designs and Patents Act, 1988.
A CIP catalogue record for this book is available from the British Library.
(hardback) 10 9 8 7 6 5 4 3 2 1
(paperback) 10 9 8 7 6 5 4 3
Printed in Singapore

Who Wants a DRAGON?

ORCHARD BOOKS

James Mayhew ✳ Lindsey Gardiner

Who wants a dragon,

all fiery and bright?

A lost baby dragon,
alone in the night?

Who wants a dragon?

This witch in a hat?

A dragon is much more fun than a cat!

But dragons are not the best thing
for a broom.

They're bigger than cats
and there's not enough room!

Who wants a dragon?

This knight brave and bold?

How could he leave him out in the cold?

But inside his helmet
the knight's in a fright.
He's certain the dragon
will give him a bite!

Who wants a dragon?

This sleeping princess?

But look out, he's got muddy paws
on her dress!

Poor little dragon, all in a muddle.

There must be someone
who'll give him a cuddle!

Who wants a dragon?

This king or his queen?

Nobody wants him,
not even this fairy.

Everyone seems to
think he's too scary!

There must be someone,
somewhere out there,

who'd cuddle a
dragon with love
to spare.

Poor little dragon,
alone in the night.

But look! Here comes someone
who'll love him just right.

His mummy!

She'll cuddle and kiss him,

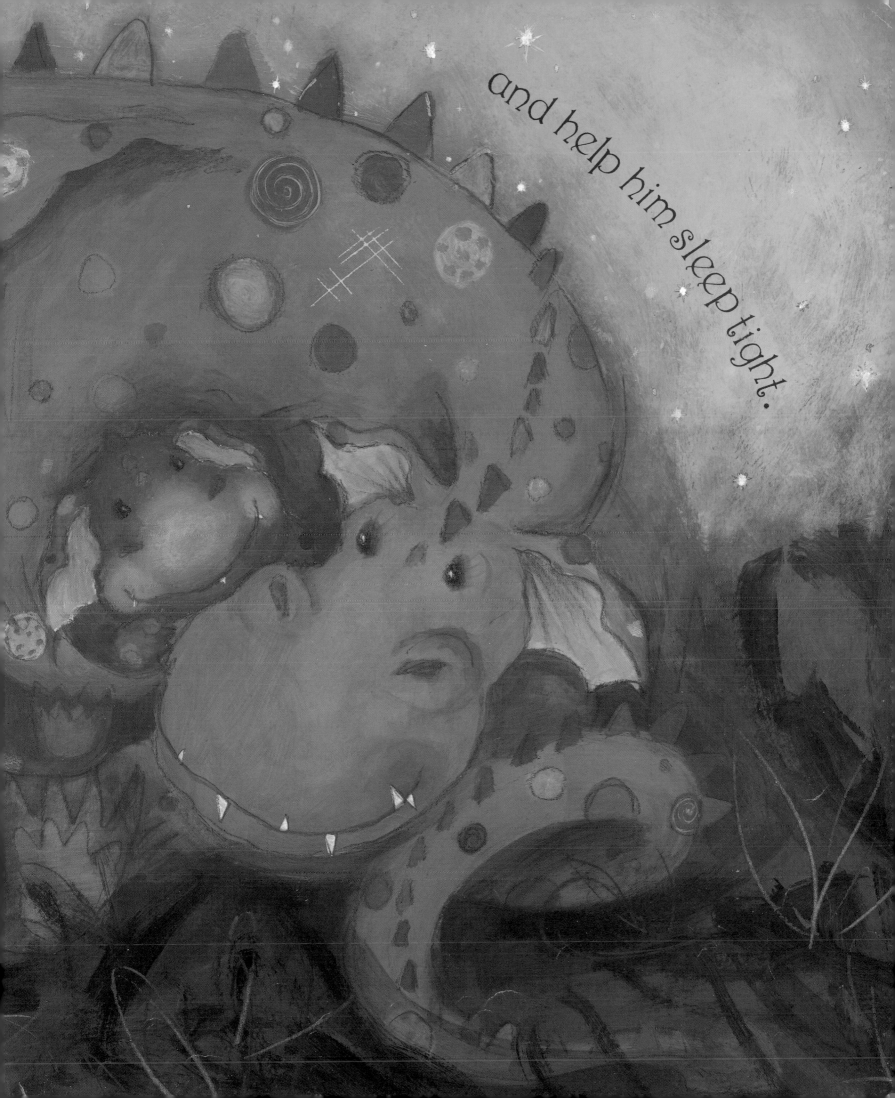

and help him sleep tight.

The End